The Skeleton in the Closet

To my very scary pair, Spence and Dylan
—A.S.

For Mum, thanks for leaving the light on. All my love.
—C.J.

The Skeleton in the Closet

Text copyright © 2003 by Alice Schertle

Illustrations copyright © 2003 by Curtis Jobling

Manufactured in China. All rights reserved.

www.harperchildrens.com

Library of Congress Cataloging-in-Publication Data

Schertle, Alice.

The skeleton in the closet / By Alice Schertle ; illustrated by Curtis
Jobling. — 1st ed.

p. cm.

Summary: A scary skeleton terrorizes a boy in his bedroom while it
searches his closet for clothes to wear.

ISBN 0-688-17738-7 — ISBN 0-688-17739-5 (lib. bdg.)

[1. Skeleton—Fiction. 2. Clothing and dress—Fiction. 3. Stories in
rhyme.] I. Jobling, Curtis, ill. II. Title.

PZ8.3.S29717 Sk 2003   2002005643

[E]—dc21   CIP

                                                              AC

Typography by Al Cetta and Drew Willis

1 2 3 4 5 6 7 8 9 10

❖

First Edition

The Skeleton in the Closet

by Alice Schertle

illustrated by Curtis Jobling

HarperCollinsPublishers

Late one night I was sound asleep,
snoring like a motorcycle, cuddled down deep
in my crocodile comforter, snug as a clam,
when I thought I heard a knocking—

BAM! BAM! BAM!

Someone at the door! I sat up straight.
Who would come a-knocking on my door so late?
In my spaceman jams I crept downstairs
and tiptoed to the window in my bedroom slipper bears.

I moved the curtain and peeked through the crack—
Two empty eyeholes stared right back!

White bones,
bright bones,
night bones glowing,
bare bones, scare bones, teeth all showing
in a big, wide, petrified, skeleton grin.

A deep-down voice said,
"Let me in!"

I ran like a rabbit.
I took the stairs
three at a time in
my bedroom slipper bears.
Into the bedroom!
Slam the door!

I stood there shaking in the middle of the floor.
Suddenly a noise made my knees grow weak—
Someone on the staircase!

creak . . . creak . . . creak . . .

Bones on the first step—
What do they want?

Second step ... third step ...
bones on a haunt,

fourth, fifth, sixth step . . .
white bones walking,

seventh step . . . eighth step . . .
night bones *talking*.

Ninth step, tenth—bones coming upstairs!
I jumped right out of my bedroom slipper bears
and dived inside of my nice safe bed
with my nice safe pillow on top of my head—
but I heard
every word
that the bone man said:

"I got a big hollow head bone,
ribs in a row,
got hip bones, thigh bones,
knee bones below,
got two shiny shin bones and little bone toes,
but I'm wearin' no skin, so EVERYTHING shows—
Comin' up to find some skeleton clothes!"

Fourteen . . . fifteen . . . very last stair. . . .

He was looking for something his bones could wear!

What did he mean by skeleton clothes?
Waterproof skin and a nose that blows?

Bones out shopping—
Good-bye skin!

The door burst open
and BONES walked in!

He walked straight to the closet and helped himself
to whatever he found on the underwear shelf:

spaceman underpants,
polka dots, plaid,
tanks and T-shirts—whatever I had,

trying on jackets, tying on ties,
buttoning buttons, zipping up flies,

rattling hangers, banging around,
trying and tossing whatever he found,

but when he came out I'd have to say
he was looking good, in a skeleton way.

He boogied across the bedroom floor,
gave me thumb-bones-up and was out the door.

He was gone at last, I don't know where,
but wherever he is, his bones aren't bare.

So . . .

if a skeleton calls on *you* tonight,

and he's wearing clothes, they're mine, all right,

but
you might not
hear him
when he climbs *your* stairs.

He'll be

quiet,

quiet,

quiet,

in my bedroom slipper bears.